Picnic

John Burningham

CANDLEWICK PRESS

First U.S. edition 2014

Library of Congress Catalog Card Number pending
ISBN 978-0-7636-6945-4

14 15 16 17 18 19 TLF 10 9 8 7 6 5 4 3 2 1

Printed in Dongguan, Guangdong, China

This book was typeset in Garamond.
The illustrations were done in paint.

Candlewick Press
99 Dover Street
Somerville, Massachusetts 02144

visit us at www.candlewick.com

Boy and Girl lived in a house
on top of a hill.

One day they made a picnic lunch.

Then they went down the hill
with the picnic basket.

At the bottom of the hill were
Sheep, Pig, and Duck.

"Come and have a picnic with us,"
said Boy and Girl.

So they all went to find a place
to have their picnic.

But they had not seen Bull.

Bull started to chase them.

Duck, Pig, Sheep, Boy, and Girl ran
as fast as they could toward
the woods to hide from Bull.

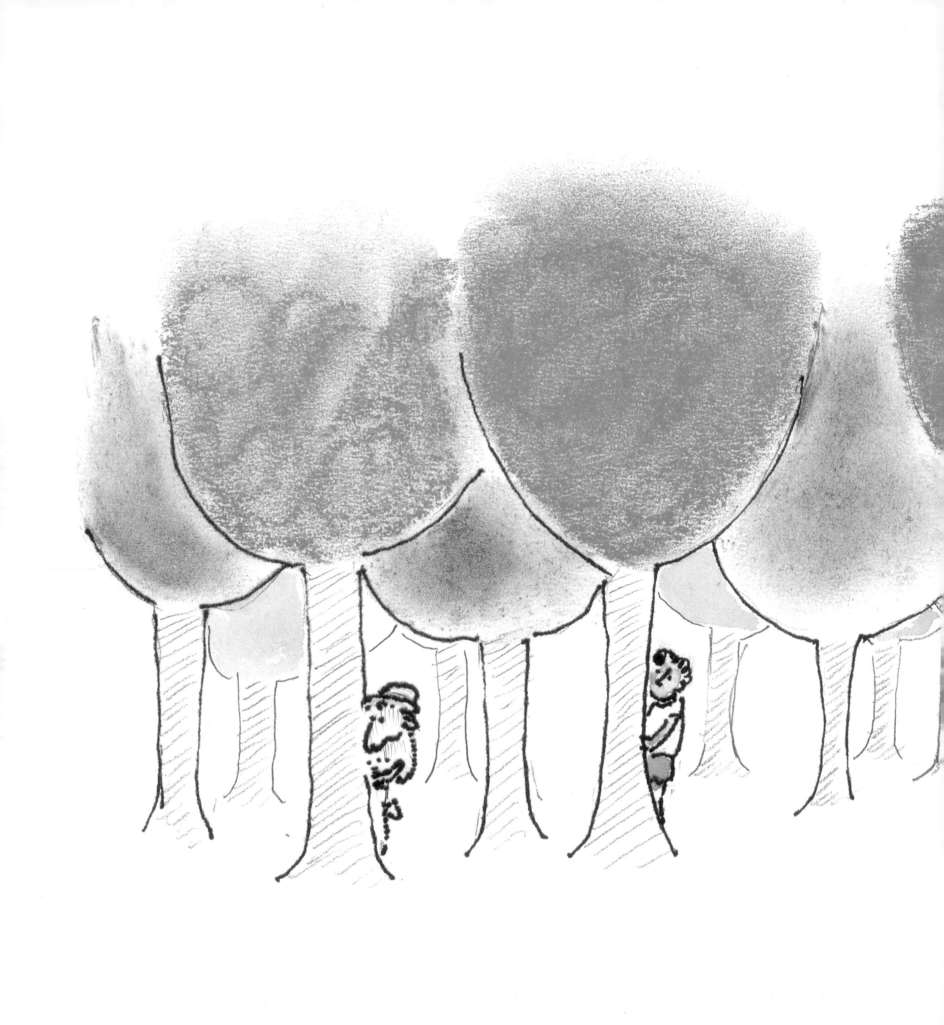

Can you find Boy, Girl, Pig, Sheep, and Duck?

After Bull went away, they came out
of the woods to have their picnic.

But the wind blew Sheep's hat away.

Can you find Sheep's hat?

Then Pig dropped his ball.
It rolled away down the hill . . .

and into a pond.
Duck went in to look for it.

Can you find Pig's ball?

They walked all over the field to
find a place for their picnic.

Then Duck lost his scarf.
Can you see it?

They were all getting very hungry.
At last they found a good place
to have their picnic.

Then they played games until it was
time to go home.

They were all very tired as they
climbed up the hill.

"You can sleep at our house," said Boy and Girl.

So Boy, Girl, Pig, Sheep, and Duck
all went to sleep.

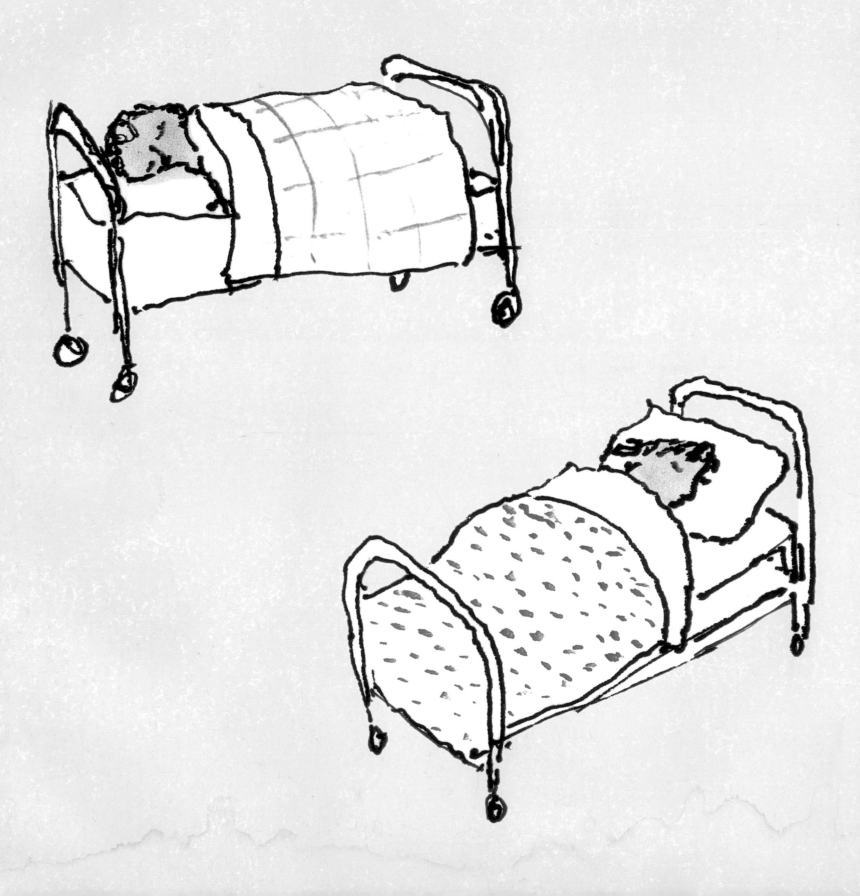

Who is sleeping in which bed?

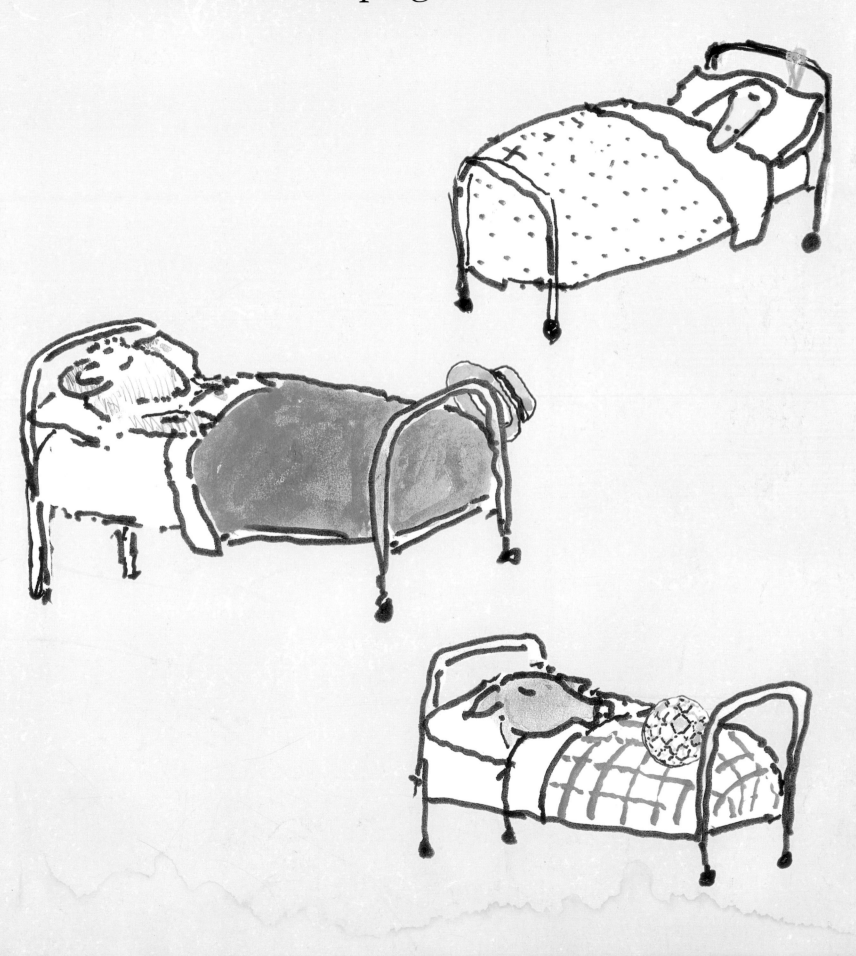

Shall we see if we can find your bed?